THE BEST FOOD

by Linda Lundberg
illustrated by Greg Schultz

Orlando   Boston   Dallas   Chicago   San Diego

Visit *The Learning Site!*
www.harcourtschool.com

Fox, Duck, and Goat walked
down a road. "I make the best
food," boasted Goat.

"No, I do," said Duck.
Fox said, "Let's all make something
to show who is the best."

"I will make a roast," said Fox.

"I will make eggs and toast," Duck said.

"I will make a big bowl
of oats," said Goat.

The animals went to Fox's
house with the food.

Fox was at the door. "I asked Toad
to try each food," said Fox. "Toad
will tell us who made the best."

"This roast is the best," croaked
Toad. "So are the eggs and toast!"

Then Toad had some oats from the
bowl. "These oats are wonderful!"
he croaked.

8

The animals all looked at Toad.
Would he tell them who made the
best dinner?

Toad croaked, "Fox
made the best roast.
Duck made the best
eggs and toast. Goat
made the best oats."

10

"We are all the best!" they said.
"Let's share our food!"

Fox said, "How kind of Toad
to tell us we are all the best!"